Embertide

Tamsin Peake

House of Sharky Press

Contents

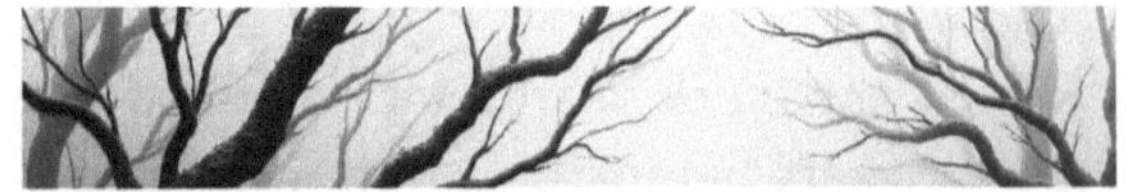

Part One:

ARRIVAL

The M40 deposited Sarah Wickham into Aylesbury on a Monday afternoon in late September, when the light had already begun its retreat toward winter. She'd driven from London with the windows down despite the chill, relishing the feel of air on her face, trying to clear her head of the hospital smell that had clung to her clothes, her hair, her skin for the past three weeks. Her mother's death had felt slow and clinical, all beeping machines and rushed video consultations, but had been short and brutal.

Nothing like the quick heart attack that had taken her father twenty years before, and with restrictions still in place for gatherings, no funeral and no family gatherings to mark her becoming an orphan. Her marriage had ended six months before, infidelity (not hers) fuelled by boredom, isolation and endless scrolling.

Sarah had channelled her grief and rage into practicality, tying up loose ends and holding at bay the question 'what now?' And in the midst of this, a letter, envelope banded in black.

The inheritance was unexpected: a house in Aylesbury she'd never known existed, left to her by a great-aunt she'd met exactly twice. The first time had been at her father's funeral, his aunt appearing in black lace and a parasol that looked Victorian, and had not stopped staring at her. She hadn't noticed, sixteen, preoccupied and in shock, but her friends had and thought she was kind of weird and cool at the same time. Great Aunt Margery had appeared once more at Sarah's university graduation five years later, pressing an old silver coin into her palm with fingers like bird bones.

"Keep this safe," she'd said, her breath smelling of peppermint and something earthier, darker. "You'll need it when the time comes."

Sarah had lost the coin within a month.

Now, at thirty-six, divorced and exhausted, she turned onto Market Street and followed the solicitor's directions to Bourbon Street. All fleeting hopes of a new start, of her own reinvention, evaporated as she exited the round-about. The name had made her think of New Orleans, of jazz and French colonialism, but this Bourbon Street was narrow and medieval, the houses leaning toward each other like conspirators, and the already overcast day seemed just a little bit darker.

The buildings looked wrong in a way she couldn't articulate - not derelict, but arranged according to some geometry that didn't match the rest of the town. Windows sat at odd heights. Doorways tilted imperceptibly. The street itself curved when it should have been straight, following some older path beneath the modern paving.

The first time the curve surprised her, she blamed her distraction, her grief. The second time, she slowed down and paid closer attention. But the street continued to defy her expectations. Her GPS kept recalculating, the blue dot jumping erratically as if confused by the geography. She tried to follow the route it suggested and found herself passing the same post box three times, approaching it from different directions each time.

The third time, she stopped the car entirely and got out, staring at the pavement. The tarmac was new, couldn't be more than a few years old, but underneath she could see the faint impression of older stones, their arrangement forming a pattern that hurt to look at directly. Not a spiral exactly, and not quite a maze, but something between the two - a configuration that suggested purpose but refused to reveal what that purpose was.

She crouched down and ran her fingers over the tarmac. It was warm, though the sun had barely touched it. And there was a texture beneath the smoothness, a sensation like the pavement was breathing, expanding and contracting with a rhythm too slow to see but possible to feel if you paid attention.

Sarah jerked her hand back and wiped it on her jeans. Glancing around for any onlookers, she took a tentative sniff. The warmth lingered on her fingers, and with it came a smell - limestone and iron and something organic, something that reminded her of aquariums, of things kept in artificial environments for too long.

She got back in the car and drove more slowly, surrendering to the street's logic rather than fighting it. The street was deserted, strange for a Monday afternoon, but Aylesbury might still have pockets locked down by the virus. The quiet had let her drive at snail's pace, carefully and slowly. This time she found Bourbon Street on the first try, as if the town had been testing her patience and was satisfied she'd learned to submit.

Number 47 stood at the end of a short terrace, its door painted an oxblood red that had weathered to the colour of dried flowers. She pushed her glasses back up from where they always slid down, as she fished for the key in her backpack.

Between settling her mum's affairs and dealing with the fallout from her divorce, her concentration was shot and she could have left it anywhere. But it was there, heavy and solid in an envelope in the front pocket. The key the solicitor had posted fit smoothly into the lock, as if it had been oiled recently. The mechanism turned with a soft click that sounded a lot like a tongue against teeth. With an involuntary moue, she turned the handle and prepared to step inside.

Inside, the house smelled of lavender and something underneath it, something that reminded Sarah of the Natural History Museum's mineral collection. Not unpleasant, but odd for a house. Wrong for anything living. She stood in the hallway for a full minute, breathing shallowly, trying to identify the scent. Limestone, she decided. Wet limestone and iron.

But there was more to it than that. The air itself felt different - heavier, denser, as if she'd descended into a basement even though she was still on the ground floor. Sound behaved strangely. Her footsteps on the floorboards echoed twice - once normally, once a fraction of a second later, as if the house was repeating them back to her.

The hallway was narrow and dark despite the afternoon light outside. The wallpaper was old but pristine, patterned with vines and flowers that Sarah didn't recognize. When she looked at them directly, they were just flowers. But in her peripheral vision, they seemed to move, to twist and reach toward each other as if completing some pattern she couldn't quite perceive.

She walked through to the sitting room and stopped in the doorway. The furniture was arranged precisely - sofa facing the fireplace, armchairs at exact angles, a coffee table centred on a rug whose pattern mimicked the one she'd seen in the street outside. Everything clean, everything in place, everything waiting.

The sofa was upholstered in fabric patterned with birds she didn't recognize, their beaks hooked and their eyes too knowing, too aware. She approached it slowly, unable to shake the feeling that she was being watched. When she touched the fabric, it was warm beneath her fingers, as if something had been sitting there moments before. The warmth spread up her arm, into her shoulder, wrapping around her like a fever. She jerked her hand back and the sensation faded, but slowly, reluctantly, as if it wanted to cling to her.

A kitchen with a Belfast sink and copper pots hanging from iron hooks, each pot's interior stained with residue she didn't want to examine closely. The stains weren't rust or food - they were darker, almost black, and they formed patterns around the circumference of each pot, as if someone had been cooking the same thing in all of them, over and over, for years.

The wooden countertops bore knife marks that formed patterns - not random, but deliberate, like tally marks or primitive writing. Hundreds of them, maybe thousands, carved deep into the wood. She ran her finger along one set of marks and felt them pulse slightly, as if the wood remembered the blade, remembered the pressure and the intent behind each cut. Some of the marks were fresh, the wood pale beneath them. Her great-aunt had died three months ago, but someone had been here since then, continuing the work, maintaining the pattern.

Upstairs, three bedrooms. The smallest was empty except for a single chair facing the window, positioned so precisely in the centre of the room that Sarah knew it had to have been measured.

She approached the window and looked out at the view: Bourbon Street curving away toward the Old Town, and in the distance, the square tower of St. Mary's Church rising above the medieval rooftops. From this angle, she could see that the church wasn't quite aligned with the other buildings - it sat at a slight angle, as if it had been built according to different principles, responding to different forces.

The middle room contained shelves lined with bottles and jars, their contents murky. Sarah switched on the light but it barely helped - the shadows in the corners seemed to resist illumination, growing darker rather than lighter when the bulb flickered to life.

The jars were labelled in her great-aunt's handwriting: dates and single words in a language Sarah didn't recognize. One said "Remembrance 1967." Another read "Acknowledgment 1973." A third, larger than the rest, was labelled simply "Before" and contained a liquid that moved against the glass, seemingly pressing toward her as she lifted it.

She left that room quickly, pulling the door shut behind her. But she imagined the things in the jars watching her through the walls, their attention following her down the hallway like a physical touch.

The largest bedroom held a four-poster bed draped in heavy curtains the blue-green of verdigris. Everything was clean, dusted, as if her great-aunt had died yesterday instead of three months ago. The bed was made with hospital corners, the pillows fluffed, a glass of water on the nightstand that was still perfectly full, no bubbles, no dust on the surface.

Sarah touched the water glass. It was cold - much colder than room temperature. And yet no condensation on the glass. When she lifted it, she saw a ring on the nightstand beneath it, a perfect circle that had stained the wood. It didn't look like water. It was darker, almost black, and it had depth to it, as if the liquid that made it had soaked down through the wood and into something deeper, something below.

She set the glass down carefully, matching it to the ring, and backed out of the room.

Someone had been maintaining this place. Someone had been here recently, keeping everything clean and ordered and ready. But the solicitor had assured her the house had been locked since Margery's death, that no one had been given keys, that Sarah was the sole heir and the first person to enter since the locks had been changed.

Sarah checked every window on the ground floor, peering out at the street. No one. The neighbouring houses showed no signs of life - no lights, no movement behind curtains. She checked her phone: 4:47 PM. People should be coming home from work, making dinner, existing.

On the kitchen table, she found an envelope with her name written in handwriting she recognized from birthday cards sent sporadically throughout her childhood. Inside, a single sheet of paper:

Sarah,
By the time you read this, I'll be gone. I've left you the house because you're the last one, and because you have a duty, though you've never known it. Your father had it too, but he left Aylesbury and left us. He thought he'd escaped. He was wrong about that, but it bought him time and brought us you.

The house will take care of you, but you must take care of it in return. There are rules. I've left my notebooks in the cellar. Read them. All of them. Don't skip ahead.

And Sarah - whatever you do, never go into the Old Town after dark during Embertide. Lock the doors. Stay inside. Wait for the bells.

I truly regret having to leave you with this. But there's no one else.

M.W.

Sarah read the letter three times, then folded it and set it back on the table.

Embertide. The ancient observance of the seasons, fasting and feasting, appropriated by early Christians. She knew the term from her History studies years ago, vaguely remembering the connection with Harvest Festivals, but why was it here? Sarah knew of some that people sometimes turned to religion in their late years - but this warning? And what was this about duty - and her father?

Her great-aunt had been old - in her nineties - and old people sometimes became confused. They'd seen it with Margery's brother, Grandpa Kevin. Dementia, Alzheimer's, one of those diseases that nibbled away at the architecture of the mind until nothing remained but fragments and fear. It was said to run in families. Her handwriting seemed coherent but had this been Great Aunt Margery's reality in her last days? Frightened and preoccupied by her own childhood terrors?

Still, Sarah found herself checking that the front door was locked before she went to find the cellar entrance. And checking it again. And a third time, pulling hard on the handle to make sure it held.

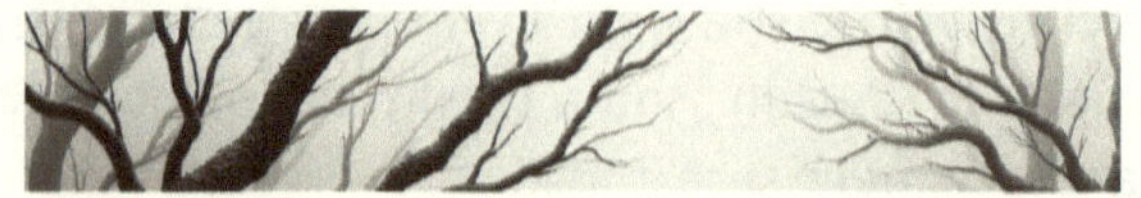

Part Two:

THE NOTEBOOKS

The cellar door was in the kitchen, behind a curtain patterned with the same strange birds as the sofa. Sarah hadn't noticed it at first - the curtain hung perfectly still despite the draft she'd felt when she'd entered the house, and when she pulled it aside, the door seemed to recede slightly, as if reluctant to be found.

The stairs descended into darkness that smelled of earth and time. Sarah flicked the light switch and a bare bulb illuminated stone walls and a packed dirt floor. The walls were older than the house above them, older than anything she'd seen in Aylesbury. The stones fit together without mortar, their surfaces carved with marks that might have been tool marks or might have been deliberate - spirals and lines that seemed to move when she wasn't looking directly at them.

Wooden shelves lined three walls, stacked with preserving jars. Sarah stepped closer to examine them and immediately regretted it. The contents were wrong. Not spoiled food or mouldy vegetables, but things that shouldn't be preserved, things that shouldn't exist.

In one jar, something that looked like a child's hand, the fingers too long and with too many joints, seven or eight per finger instead of three. The skin was pale and wrinkled from the preserving liquid, but the fingernails were dark and sharp, more like claws. And at the wrist, instead of ending cleanly, the flesh extended into tendrils that moved slowly through the liquid, exploring the glass, leaving trails of something dark behind them.

"What the...?"

In another jar, a substance that might have been honey but swirled as if by itself against the glass with obvious intent, forming shapes - faces, mouths, reaching hands - that seemed pressed against the glass as Sarah approached, as if recognizing her, as if wanting something from her.

A third jar contained what appeared to be teeth, dozens of them, all different sizes and shapes. Some were recognizably human - molars and incisors and canines. But others were wrong. Too large, or too small, or shaped for purposes Sarah couldn't identify. One tooth was spiraled like a narwhal's tusk. Another split at the end into three points, each point serrated. A cluster of tiny teeth, no bigger than grains of rice, were fused together into a structure that looked almost like coral, almost like a brain.

Another jar held what might have been a tongue, pale and bloated, covered in …Mouths? Sarah peered through the dim light at what looked impossibly like tiny mouths that opened and closed in unison, each one revealing a throat that went down impossibly far, down past where a throat should end, down into darkness that seemed to have no bottom. The liquid it floated in was clear but too thick, moving like glycerine.

As she turned away, she caught a glimpse of movement. All the tiny mouths turned toward her simultaneously, and she stepped back so quickly she knocked over a stack of newspapers behind her.

The papers scattered across the dirt floor - dozens of them, maybe a hundred, all copies of the Aylesbury Vale

News spanning decades. Sarah picked one up with shaking hands. October 1959. The headline read "Search Continues for Missing Boy." Below it was a photograph of Thomas Carver, a thin child with dark hair and a serious expression. He was holding a model airplane and smiling uncertainly, as if the photographer had told him a joke he didn't quite understand.

She picked up another paper. October 1966: "Local Girl Still Missing After Week." Emma Pritchard, sixteen, wearing a sundress and squinting into the sun. Another: September 1973: "Family Pleads for Return of Adopted Son." David Chen, twelve, solemn and careful in a school photograph.

Every paper marked a disappearance. Her great-aunt had kept them all, had documented every single one, had created an archive of the missing that stretched back seven decades. Scanning through them, Sarah noticed the same months recurring.

She set the papers down and forced herself to examine more of the jars. One contained something that looked like a preserved foetus, but with too many limbs arranged in spirals around its torso, and a face that wasn't quite a face - the features were there but positioned wrong, as if someone had assembled them from memory without quite understanding how they fit together.

Another held what appeared to be eyes - dozens of them, all different sizes and colours and species. Human eyes. Cat eyes? Eyes that belonged to things Sarah had no names for, with pupils shaped like stars or squares or spirals. All suspended in fluid that caught the cellar light and refracted it into rainbow patterns. When she moved, the eyes seemed to track her, following her motion through the glass, their gazes converging on her with an intensity that made her skin crawl.

The largest jar sat on the bottom shelf, almost hidden behind the others. It was made of very old glass, greenish and irregular, the kind you see in museums. The label had faded almost completely, but Sarah could make out a single word in archaic handwriting: "First."

Inside was something Sarah's mind struggled to process. It looked organic - tissue, membrane, something that might once have been internal organs. But it was arranged wrong, structured according to geometries that made her eyes water and her stomach clench. It had folds that went inward forever, surfaces that were both convex and concave simultaneously, edges that seemed to exist in more than three dimensions. Every time she tried to focus on it, her vision blurred and her head began to ache, and somewhere deep in her ears, she heard a sound like water draining, like something large and wet moving through a narrow space.

"What the hell were you into, Great Aunt Margery?" She muttered.

She backed away from the shelves and turned to the small desk in the corner. A stack of leather-bound notebooks sat there, each labelled with dates spanning decades. The earliest was dated 1952, the most recent from three months ago.

Sarah carried them upstairs, her hands shaking so badly she nearly dropped them twice on the narrow stairs. Her ex-wife used to joke about her lack of imagination, but combination of the light, the oppressive air and the weirdness of that subterranean larder had seriously rattled her, and she shut the door behind her with relief. She spread the books across the kitchen table and opened the first one.

January 1st, 1952. Mother is dead. I'm twenty-three years old and the responsibility has fallen to me. Mrs. Beckett from the church brought round a casserole and told me she was sorry for my loss, but her eyes said other things. She knows what I am now. What I have to be.

Father used to say there were thirteen families in the Old Town, and ours was the oldest. We've been here since before the printing press, since before the Black Death, since before the Normans built their tower. We were here when this was just a spring and a circle of stones, when the people spoke a language that has no name anymore.

As she poked around in the kitchen to find a mug and make tea, Sarah thought about her great aunt sitting at this table in her empty house, fridge full of bereavement casseroles and contemplating what came next. The idea that Great Aunt Margery's - and her - family had such deep roots in this town was bewildering. She sat back down and carried on reading. More notes about families and names that meant nothing to Sarah, and then -

Our job - my job now - is the keeping. That's what Mother called it. The keeping of the old agreements, the old bargains. Because something lives in the spring beneath Aylesbury, and it has lived there longer than churches or councils or any authority we'd recognize. And every seven years, it requires acknowledgment.

Sarah closed the notebook and looked out the window. The street was still empty. The light was failing rapidly now, the sun setting earlier than it should in September. She checked her phone: 5:34 PM. But the quality of the darkness outside suggested much later, closer to eight or nine.

She turned on every light on the ground floor before opening the next notebook.

Her great-aunt's handwriting remained steady and precise across decades, documenting meetings with people Sarah assumed were other members of these thirteen families, describing rituals performed at specific days of the Ember Week, recording the years when the keeping was required.

The entries became increasingly detailed as the years progressed, as if Margery had needed to document everything, to leave a complete record of what she'd done and why.

September 28th, 1959. Embertide begins tomorrow. The others are ready. We've chosen the Carver boy this time - the one with the twisted foot who'll never work in his father's shop. His parents were relieved when we asked, though they tried to hide it. They understood. Everyone in the Old Town understands, even if they don't say it aloud.

This is the mercy of it, Mother always said. We choose those who'll be missed the least, whose absence will cause the least suffering, and whose lives would be hardship. We choose those who are already marked, already separate. The spring accepts the gift and the town is safe for another seven years.

A sudden hoot at the window made her jump with a sharp squeal. An owl. This was ridiculous. She was getting spooked at nothing, just an old lady's stories.

I led him down myself on the last night. He was fright-ened but he went willingly enough once I gave him the draft. The words came easier this time, flowed from my tongue like water. The spring was hungry. I could feel it through the stones, through my bones. Thomas walked into the water and the spring embraced him.

He sank without a sound. The water didn't even ripple.

Sarah stood up so quickly her chair fell backward. The crash echoed through the empty house, and for an instant she thought she heard an answering sound from the cellar - a wet sliding noise, like something large and moist, shifting in confined space.

She picked up the chair with trembling hands and sat down again. This couldn't be real. Fantasy, delusion, the ramblings of a woman who'd lived too long in isolation and grief. The dates were specific. The names could be real. She could check, couldn't she? Look up the old news, see if a Carver boy had actually gone missing in 1959.

Her laptop was still in her car. Sarah went to get it, stepping out into the gathering dark. The temperature had dropped at least ten degrees since she'd arrived. Her breath misted in front of her face.

The cats had appeared. Seven of them sat in a precise semicircle around her car, all black or dark gray, all watching her with identical yellow eyes. They didn't move as she approached, didn't scatter when she unlocked the door. They just watched. And when she glanced back at the house, she saw more cats on the windowsills, on the doorsteps, on the roof tiles. Dozens of them, all facing her.

Sarah grabbed her laptop and fled back inside, slamming the door and throwing both locks. Her hands were ice-cold and wouldn't stop shaking. She made another tea, replacing the earlier one left undrunk. She opened her laptop with fingers that felt disconnected from her body.

The British News Archives went back centuries. She searched for "Carver 1959 missing" and found it halfway down the page :

October 2nd, 1959: Local Boy Missing
Thomas Carver, 8, of Market Street, has been reported missing by his parents. Thomas, who walks with a pronounced limp due to a birth defect, was last seen on the evening of September 29th near St. Mary's Church. Police are asking anyone with information to come forward.

There was no follow-up article. Sarah scrolled through the subsequent weeks, the months after. Nothing. Thomas Carver had simply vanished, and the town had moved on.

She spent the next four hours cross-referencing the names and dates in her great-aunt's notebooks with the local news archives. The pattern was there, undeniable and meticulous. Every seven years, September, during the four days of the Michaelmas Embertide - someone disappeared in Aylesbury.

Always young, children most of them. Always in some way marked as different or vulnerable. Every single one a cold case with no further mention, as though swallowed by quicksand or consensus.

1959: Thomas Carver, 8, with a club foot.
1966: Emma Pritchard, 16, described in her great-aunt's notes as "simple-minded."

1973: David Chen, 12, the adopted son of the Chinese restaurant owners on Cambridge Street.

1980: Sarah Morrison, 15, pregnant.

1987: Shane O'Riordan, 16, "the Irish boy who came here thinking he could hide from his troubles."

1994: Aisha Kaur, 9, "the Sikh girl whose family didn't understand our ways."

The pages for 2001 were missing. Sarah rifled though a few of the notebooks to see if any loose pages fell out. She examined the book more closely, finding small shreds at the crease, evidence of pages carefully eased out of their stitching. Filing this as 'something to come back to later', she read on.

2008: Lily Peterson, 13, "the transgender child whose parents had already given up."

And then … there it was. Under a folded newspaper article about the continued search for Lily. A single line dated three months prior to the girl's disappearance.

"After 2001. After what I let happen to Harry. My only nephew. I can't refuse again."

And then after a few more clippings appealing for information about Lily, from 2008, the next year – nothing. Sarah looked for 2015: Nobody. There was no new name in this terrible list. The line in her great-aunt's notebook had simply read: *I'm too old. I can't do this anymore. I'm going to break the chain. Forgive me.*

Sarah reread that entry. Her great-aunt's handwriting wavered there, the letters shaky and uncertain. And below it, added later in darker ink: *I was wrong to think mercy would matter. I was stupid to think it would understand.*

Then nothing. Pages smeared with ink and smudges, no words. Sarah flipped the pages and almost missed the final entry towards the end of the notebook:

June 3rd, 2022. The signs have been showing. The spring water tastes of copper and the birds have stopped singing in the Old Town. I made my decision seven years ago and the debt has been accumulating. Something will happen this Embertide. Something must.

I've made arrangements for Sarah. Now that Harry's gone, she's the only one left with the bloodline, the only one who might be able to make it right. I should have prepared her. Should have brought her here when I had the chance, when she was young enough to learn the ways.

I should have told her when Harry died. About us, about how her father ran when my brother died, how we hoped he would be safe and forgotten, far away from here – and how I let my nephew die. But I was a coward. and I couldn't face her. I couldn't tell her it was my fault. And now here I am again. Too weak to do what's needed.

The spring is waiting. We know it. And the bones have chosen me. Again.

But I can't. My hands shake too much. My bones ache with the weight of it. Every morning I wake up tasting lime-stone and iron, and I know it's calling me home. So I will pay the debt myself and hope that it is enough.

Sarah, if you're reading this - I'm sorry. I failed and I'm so very sorry.

Sarah checked the date on her phone: September 19th 2022. She flipped through the notebooks, found the calendar her great-aunt had maintained, meticulous notations for every year going back to 1952.

Embertide this year began on September 21st - two days from now - and ran through to September 24th.

She should leave. Put her things back in her car, drive somewhere - anywhere - and never return. Let the solicitor deal with selling the house. Let Aylesbury and its spring and its nightmare traditions sink back into whatever dark age had spawned them.

But even as she thought this, other thoughts were tugging at her attention. Her dad had died in 2002. Her dad had run from this place and it hadn't saved him.

He'd died at thirty-seven of a heart attack his doctors couldn't explain, a man who ran five kilometres every morning and ate brown bread, dying in the middle of the night with no warning, no pain, no reason.

And there was something else. Something she'd been ignoring since she'd entered the house: a feeling of recognition. As if the house and the street and even the watching cats were familiar to her in some way she couldn't access. As if she'd been here before, in some life or dream she couldn't quite remember.

She found blankets in the hall cupboard and made a nest on the couch, covering the strange birds with the familiar sensations of wool and cotton. She couldn't bring herself to venture upstairs and sleep in the crisply arranged four poster. Not tonight.

Turning off the kitchen light and rechecking the front door, she balanced some toast on a cup of tea and carried the notebooks to the lounge, where she prepared to reread her Great Aunt Margery's story.

By dawn, she understood what her great-aunt had been, what she had done for seven decades. And what Sarah was now expected to do.

The families who'd maintained the keeping were mostly gone. Some had died out, their children leaving Aylesbury for lives elsewhere. Others had simply stopped partici- pating and just seemed to vanish, with with no further mention made of them.

According to the most recent entries, only three of the original thirteen families remained: the Wickhams - now just Sarah - the Harrows, and the Beckers.

There were instructions for the ritual, detailed and spe- cific. The coyly termed 'gift' had to be brought to the spring at midnight on the final night of Embertide. They had to be bound but conscious, had to be able to walk of their own will down the steps that led beneath St. Mary's Church to the place where the spring rose from deep rock.

Instructions for the drink that would make them calm, compliant. The words that had to be spoken were written in a language Sarah didn't recognize. Her great-aunt had thoughtfully included phonetic translations.

And there were consequences for failing to give the gift. Her great-aunt had documented them carefully:

1940 - The Thompsons decided they couldn't participate anymore. Called it barbaric, called us murderers. Two years after that Embertide, their house collapsed. Sinkhole, the authorities said. The whole family gone in a moment. I was just a girl. But I saw the earth swallow that house. I saw it happen, I know I did. It looked like the earth was starving.

1945 - After the war, people were different. The Martins said we couldn't keep doing this, that Hitler's ovens had shown us where this kind of thinking led. It was their turn, but they wouldn't help choose. Not even after the Thompsons! That November, the spring flooded. Just that one spring, nowhere else.

The water came up through the church crypt and it was black and it stank of things long dead. The Martins' youngest, Alice, went missing. They found her in the flooded crypt, drowned but with no water in her lungs. I head Mother tell Father she made a sound like a half full milk bottle when they moved her, liquid sloshing in her skull like it was looking for a way out.

Sarah thought again about the missing pages for the year before her father's death and Great Aunt Margery's desperate apology for - what? She closed the notebook as the sun rose over Bourbon Street, painting the red door gold. The light looked wrong, too thick, oozing across the wood like treacle, unstoppable and seductive. The next day would be the start of this year's Embertide and seven years after the last ritual. And somehow she was at the centre of whatever Lovecraftian horror story her great aunt had been writing about all these years.

She had one day to decide what to do. She would start by getting some answers answers from the Old Town.

Part
Three:

THE OLD TOWN

September 20th. The day before Embertide.

Sarah had spent the morning walking through Aylesbury, trying to understand the geography of what her great-aunt had documented. The modern town centre was bright and commercial - chain stores and coffee shops, the usual homogenization of English market towns.

Normal people cautiously returning to their normal lives, making the most of the freedom to buy bread and coffee and magazines, completely unaware of what lay beneath their feet. Or perhaps they knew and had learned not to think about it, the dread and uncertainty of the last few years solidifying their will to look away from the wrongness at the edges of their vision.

She watched them for a while, sitting on a bench outside Boots with her rapidly cooling coffee. A mother with a pram, cooing at her baby. Two teenagers arguing about football. An elderly man feeding pigeons. All of them moving through their day with the comfortable assumption that the world was returning to rights, that cause followed effect, that horror was something that happened in other places to other people.

But tucked behind Market Square, accessible through narrow passages that seemed to resist being found, was the Old Town.

The transition was abrupt. One moment Sarah was on a well-lit pedestrian street lined with familiar chain stores, the next she was in a passage barely wide enough for her shoulders, the walls so close she could touch both sides at once. The passage curved and twisted, and when she emerged, she was somewhere else entirely.

This was where the medieval street plan remained, where buildings leaned against each other, their timber frames exposed like ribs under rotting flesh. The streets here didn't follow any logic that Sarah understood. They curved and doubled back, connected to each other in ways that made no sense when she tried to trace them on her phone's map. The GPS kept losing signal, the blue dot drifting aimlessly or jumping from one location to another with no regard for the actual path she walked.

She tried to maintain her bearings by the church tower - St. Mary's was visible from almost everywhere in the Old Town - but even that seemed to move. Sometimes it was directly ahead of her, sometimes to her left, sometimes she'd swear it was behind her though she hadn't turned around.

The buildings themselves were wrong. Not derelict - many were clearly inhabited, with curtains in the windows and lights in the rooms beyond. But they were arranged according to principles that had nothing to do with modern town planning.

Windows at odd heights, some placed so low they would have opened directly onto the street at ankle level. Doors that were too narrow or too wide, framed with lintels carved with symbols Sarah didn't recognize - not quite Christian crosses, not quite pagan runes, but something between or beyond both.

And the street names: Temple Street, Friar's Street, Kingsbury, Parsons Fee. Names that suggested religious authority and medieval power structures. But also other streets with names that made no sense: Water Lane though there was no water visible, Silent Street though Sarah could hear traffic from the modern town just a few hundred yards away, Crooked Way though it ran straight as an arrow.

The few people she saw moved quickly, heads down, as if trying not to draw attention. When she passed them, they didn't make eye contact. And there was something about their faces - nothing she could put her finger on, but a quality she recognized from her great-aunt's photographs. A wariness. An awareness. The look of people who knew something was watching and had learned to pretend they didn't notice.

St. Mary's Church sat at the heart of it all, its square tower Norman and stolid, built from pale stone that looked white in the morning light but was already greying as clouds moved across the sun. The churchyard was old, headstones tilted and illegible, yew trees older than the church itself spreading their dark canopy over forgotten graves.

Sarah paused at the churchyard gate. It was wrought iron, ornate with vines and flowers that on closer inspection revealed themselves to be bones and skulls worked into the pattern with Victorian restraint. She'd seen similar gates at other churches - a common Gothic Revival affec-tation. But these bones looked too real, too detailed. And the flowers had thorns that were too sharp, too numerous, forming patterns that made her eyes hurt when she tried to follow them.

Sarah found the Harrow family bakery on Temple Street - another name that suggested older, stranger purpos-es. The shop was open, warm light spilling out onto the pavement. Through the window she could see a woman arranging loaves in a wicker basket. When their eyes met, Sarah felt something click into place, like a key turning in a lock she hadn't known was there.

The woman came to the door and opened it. She was perhaps sixty, with grey hair pulled back in a practical bun and hands dusted with flour. Her eyes grey and sharp above her mask. "You're Margery's girl," she said. Not a question.

"Great-niece. Sarah Wickham."

"Catherine Harrow." She stepped back to let Sarah in. The shop smelled of yeast and cinnamon, but under-neath it was that same mineral smell Sarah had noticed in her great-aunt's house. "I suppose you've read the note-books."

"Some of them."
"And you're wondering if your great-aunt was insane, or if we all are."

Sarah didn't deny it. She couldn't.

Catherine gestured to a small table in the corner, away from the window. "Sit. I'll make tea. And then I'll tell you what I know, which isn't everything, but it's enough to keep you from running. If you're planning to run."

The tea was strong and sweet, sweetened with honey that tasted faintly of chalk. Sarah noticed but said nothing. Catherine sat across from her and folded her flour-dusted hands on the table.

"My grandmother told me the story when I was sixteen. She said every generation needs to understand, needs to carry the knowledge. Even if we hope they'll never need to use it."

"The spring," Sarah said.
"The spring," Catherine nodded.

"There's a cave system beneath Aylesbury. Limestone, riddled with passages and underground streams. One of them surfaces in the crypt of St. Mary's - you can see it if you know where to look, though they keep it grated over now. The water is perfectly clear and perfectly cold, and people used to think it had healing properties. Probably why the first church was built here, way back before records."

"That's not quite true though, is it?"

Catherine's expression didn't change. "Something lives in it. Or something exists there that we might as well call alive, though it's not like us. Not like anything we'd recognize. My grandmother said it was old when the Romans came, old when the Celts came. Old enough that there's no story of its beginning."

"And it demands human sacrifice."

"It demands acknowledgment," Catherine corrected gently. "That's how my grandmother put it. The spring keeps the town safe - the buildings don't fall, the floods don't come, the harvests are good. Not lucky, you understand. Actually good, year after year, in defiance of probability. But like any relationship, it requires maintenance. And every seven years, during Embertide, it requires more."

Sarah wrapped her hands around her mug. The warmth didn't reach her bones. "My great aunt stopped. Seven years ago. Why?"

"She was eighty- six years old," Catherine said quietly. "Her hands shook so badly she couldn't hold a teacup without spilling. How was she supposed to bind someone and lead them down those steps? And besides - " She paused, choosing her words.

"The world changed. Used to be, a child with a disability was hidden away, barely counted as human. A pregnant girl was ruined, worthless. Someone different - the wrong color, the wrong religion, the wrong way of loving - they weren't protected by law or custom. So when one of them disappeared, people looked the other way. Neighbors would nod and say it was a shame but probably a blessing too, and life went on."

"Lily Peterson," Sarah said. "The trans kid in 2008. She was the last one."

Catherine shifted her gaze. "The last one, yes. Margery chose her because she thought - well, we all thought - that the parents wouldn't fight too hard, that the town would shrug it off as a runaway. Maybe a suicide."

Seeing Sarah's expression she gave a slight shrug.

"Children can be so cruel. We were wrong. We hadn't bargained for social media, and times really have changed. They searched for months. There were vigils, news coverage, Facebook groups."

"It was the final straw for Margery. She kept saying she could hear the girl calling from the spring, saying she could feel her down there in the dark, still alive but not alive, still present but not conscious. It was the longest seven years of her life. "

"And with everything that happened to your father, it was too much. When it came to the next time in 2015, she couldn't do it again. She just couldn't."

Sarah started. "Wait, what about my father? She'd said it was her fault but ..."

"Yes, heart attack, wasn't it? So sad, so young." Her eyes slid to the door.

"Yes! But - Catherine, what has this got to do with my father? What did my great aunt do?"

Catherine's face folded in on itself, eyes turning to steel. Sarah thought she could see cogs turning behind them. Catherine drooped, ever so slightly. Eyes softening she looked at Sarah.

"It's what she didn't do, Sarah. In 2001 the bones called for Margery. We'd chosen, a little boy, an orphan. Who knows how he got placed here. Anyway, she was the one bidden to gather, prepare and give him to the spring on the final night of Embertide " She put up a hand to fend off interruption.

"She couldn't do it. Just something about him that made him different to the others. I mean, they're always different. But this boy. It was hard for us, too. We moved mountains to get him rehomed, far away, we agreed we, Margery, had to find ... a replacement."

Sarah watched her, a faint ringing in her ears growing louder as she followed where this was going.

"Sparrows started attacking children, there was an awful smell from the drains when the snows melted. Craters appeared in the golf course. We knew we were being warned. We hadn't found another - gift - but then it just stopped. And then we heard about your father."

She seemed to sink further into herself, and then reinflate as she eyed Sarah.

"Your great aunt never talked about Harry's death. Never mentioned him again after 2001. It broke her heart. She made the decision to spare that child, but we had all agreed. We failed the spring and it chose its own price for that. We did that. But her bloodline paid. And now you're the last, and it's happening again."

"What do you mean? What's been happening?"

"Small things, at first. A few sinkholes that got blamed on old limestone workings. Some flooding that shouldn't have happened. Nothing catastrophic." Catherine paused. "Until the Spring equinox."

Seeing Sarah's confusion she continued.

"It were six months ago. The building next to my house developed cracks. Huge ones, foundation to roof. The structural engineer said he'd never seen anything like it. Said the foundation stones looked like they'd been gnawed on." Catherine's hands tightened on her mug.

"When Margery died we thought - we thought things would be alright. That the debt was paid. But last month we had a child born with no eyelids. The cats are back. And the water in the spring has changed. It smells wrong. Tastes wrong."

"My husband went down to the crypt last week to check the grate - we take turns, the three families, making sure everything's secure - and he said the water was higher than it's ever been. And it was warm."

Sarah thought about the mineral smell in her great-aunt's house, in this bakery. "What does this all mean?"

"It's a warning. It means the spring is waking up. And when it's fully awake ... " Catherine stopped. Shook her head. Swallowed.

"My grandmother told me a story. Said there was a time, centuries ago, when the keeping stopped. A plague had killed most of the families, and there were very few left who remembered the agreements. Fewer people to spare."

"The town survived, but barely. People went mad. Children were born wrong - not disabled, but wrong, with extra bones or missing organs or mouths that grew in places mouths shouldn't be. Animals, too. And the spring itself changed. Started producing water that made you sick if you drank it, that killed plants, that drove animals away."

"The townsfolk used everything they could find to understand the terms. They drew up a covenant so that it would never happen again. It took 30 years of following the rules to restore the balance."

The cheeks behind her mask creased in a smile, the warmth not reaching her eyes. " And here we are."
"You're saying if we don't - if I don't - "

"I'm saying Margery has broken a chain that had held for seven hundred years. She'd tried before, she paid. You - her family - you all paid for that. But now, even her death hasn't been enough. You carry her debt. She thought that she could make it right. But she ran out time"
"And the spring had been patient. It had waited almost seven years. But it won't wait any longer. This Embertide, something's going to happen. Something big."

"Either you honour the agreement, or the spring will take payment from us all. And it won't be kind about it."

Sarah stood up. Her legs felt unsteady, as if the earth beneath the bakery had turned liquid.

"This isn't my problem. I didn't know anything about this before yesterday. This is insane"

Catherine gave her a hard , tight smile. "Your dad ran. Margery let him. See how that ended. You have until tomorrow night at sundown. Embertide begins then."

Catherine stood as well, but she didn't try to stop Sarah from leaving.

"Whatever you decide, be at St. Mary's at eleven tomorrow night. Becker will be there. We can at least show you the spring, let you see it for yourself. Let you understand what you're dealing with."

"And if I don't come?"

"Then you'll be making a decision anyway."

Catherine's voice was gentle, pitying. "The spring knows. It doesn't care whether you acknowledge it willingly or not. It only cares that you acknowledge it."
Outside, the afternoon light was already failing. September days were short and getting shorter as they approached the Equinox, also tomorrow. It seemed that the year was sliding toward darkness with increasing velocity, and that the next few days were a primitive stew of superstition and arcane beliefs. Sarah walked back through the

Old Town, paying attention now to details she'd missed before.

The way certain buildings had no windows facing the street. The crosses carved into lintels above doorways, protection against something that predated Christianity. The absence of birds, even pigeons, even crows. And the people - the few she saw - moved quickly, heads down, as if trying not to draw attention.

And from somewhere beneath her feet, so faint she might have imagined it, came the sound of running water.

Sarah went home, locked the door and waited for night to fall.

But night didn't fall normally. It rose. She watched from the lounge window, once more her makeshift bedroom, as darkness seeped up from the streets, from between the paving stones, from the cracks in the old buildings. It rose like water filling a basement, slow and inexorable, swallowing the light one layer at a time.

The cats returned at sunset. More than before. Dozens of them, filling Bourbon Street from end to end, all sitting in perfect rows like an audience waiting for a performance to begin. They all faced her house. They all watched her window.

Sarah closed the curtains, but she could feel them out there. Watching. Waiting.

She went back to the notebooks and read until her eyes burned.

Part Four:

EMBERTIDE

S undown on September 21st came at six-forty-two.
Sarah watched from her bedroom window as the
streetlights flickered on, their orange glow painting Bourbon Street in tones of rust and dried blood.

But the darkness that rose from the streets was thicker
than normal darkness, more substantial. It moved with

purpose, flowing around the pools of lamplight like water around stones.

The cats had already begun to gather. Not dozens this time - hundreds. They filled every available space: doorways, windowsills, parked cars, rooftops. All black or dark gray, all sitting perfectly still, all facing the same direction: southeast, toward the Old Town and the church.

Her phone buzzed with a text from an unknown number:

Sarah. Meet us at St. Mary's at eleven. Back entrance, by the yew trees. - C

Four hours to decide what she believed, what she would do.
Sarah went down to the cellar.

She'd avoided it since that first visit, had tried to pretend those jars didn't exist, that she hadn't seen what was in them. But she needed to understand. Needed to know exactly what her great-aunt had been doing down here for seven decades.

The stairs seemed steeper than before, the darkness at the bottom more complete. The bare bulb cast shadows that didn't match the objects creating them. Sarah forced herself to approach the shelves.

The jars were worse up close. What she'd thought was a child's hand was actually a hand with too many joints, the fingers bending in ways fingers shouldn't. The honey-like substance pressed against the glass, forming shapes - mouths, eyes, reaching tendrils that left trails of something dark behind them.

And the teeth. Oh God, the teeth.

They weren't just different sizes. They were different species, different kinds of things. Some were recognizably mammalian. Others had ridges and serrations she'd never seen before. And at the back of the jar, partially hidden, were teeth that looked almost human except for the way they spiraled, forming structures that couldn't possibly fit in a mouth.

Sarah backed away and her foot struck something. A box, wooden, older than anything else in the cellar. She knelt and opened it.

Inside were bones. Small ones, arranged in careful patterns. And beneath them, wrapped in muslin that fell apart at her touch, were photographs.

Black and white, faded, but clear enough. The first showed a group of people standing at the entrance to a cave, holding lanterns. Formal clothing, Victorian or Edwardian.

Their faces were serious, composed. Except for their eyes. Even in the old photograph, even through the grain and fading, their eyes were wrong. Too dark, or too light, too detailed and alive for the old technology.

The second photograph showed the interior of a chamber. Stone walls, a pool of water. And reflected in the water, something that made Sarah's vision blur, made her equilibrium shift. In the sudden flood of vertigo she she couldn't help but close her eyes.
When she opened them again, the photograph was different. The thing in the water was in a different position. As if it had moved while she wasn't looking.

She dropped the photographs back into the box, catching sight of other horrors as they fell. Forms with multi angled limbs, a picture of a stone cross that seemed to pulse and twist. She shoved to her feet and ran upstairs.

She spent the next three hours alternating between pacing and reading. She searched the web for local history from the time of no tithing that Catherine had told her about.
There it was. Folkloric accounts of spates of deformities, earthquakes, blight and pestilence that befell Aylesbury in Post - Plague years, that seemed to just stop.
She reread the journals for a clue, anything, that would make this just a stupid story, make Catherine and Margery simple rural folk with rampant imaginations. The more she read about this town, the stronger the feeling of

knowing, and with it, yearning. And when she noticed that, she paced harder.

She pulled up Kim's profile, closed the app, reloaded it. But her ex had made it very clear that she was done with Sarah and was probably busy with her new lover anyway.

Sarah was on her own. She had no one and no one from her old life knew she was here, or cared. But there was something here she needed to deal with and the minutes were dragging her there whether she wanted to or not.

At ten-thirty, she put on her jacket and walked toward the Old Town.

The streets were empty in a way that felt deliberate rather than coincidental or even explicable by post lock-down inertia. No cars, no pedestrians, no teenagers hanging around the off-license or couples snogging in the park.

Even the cats had vanished. Sarah's footsteps echoed off the old buildings, and when she turned onto Temple Street, she saw why.

Every window in the Old Town was dark, every door closed. But on each threshold sat a small bowl containing bread and - was that salt? Some white stuff and something red - berries, perhaps, or wine. And painted on the stones beside each door was a symbol Sarah recognized from her great-aunt's notebooks: a circle with three wavy lines through it, the ancient sign for water.

But the symbols were wet. Fresh. And as she watched, one of them moved, the lines shifting like living things, like veins pulsing beneath skin. She hurried past, hugging her jacket closer around her throat.

The churchyard gate was unlocked. Sarah pushed through and followed the path between listing head-stones toward the back of St. Mary's, where the yew trees grew so close to the building that their roots had cracked the foundation stones.

She could see two figures waiting beneath the largest tree: Catherine Harrow and a man who could only be one of the Beckers.

He was younger than Sarah expected - perhaps forty, with the kind of face that suggested both intelligence and something broken underneath. When she approached, he extended his hand.

"Daniel Becker. You're Sarah."

"Yes."

"I'm sorry about Margery. She was a good woman, given what she had to do." His palm was cold, his grip brief.

"I'm not sure I would describe any of this as good."

"No," Daniel agreed. "But necessary, maybe. That's what we tell ourselves."

Catherine gestured toward a low door in the back of the church, almost hidden behind ivy. "It's unlocked. We have about fifteen minutes before bell toll."

"I haven't decided - " Sarah started.

"We know," Catherine said. "We're not asking you to. We're just showing you. After that, whatever you choose is your choice."

The door opened onto narrow stone steps descending into darkness. Daniel produced a torch and led the way, Catherine following and Sarah bringing up the rear.

The steps were steep and worn smooth by centuries of feet, and the walls were close enough that Sarah could touch both sides at once. The air grew colder as they descended, and that mineral smell intensified - not sulfur exactly, but something older, darker. The smell of deep earth and slow time.

The steps ended in a low-ceilinged chamber that might once have been a crypt. Stone shelves lined the walls, empty now but shaped for holding the dead. In the centre of the room, a hole in the floor about three feet across, covered by an iron grate green with verdigris.

And from that hole came the sound of running water, echoing up from depths Sarah couldn't estimate.

Daniel knelt beside the grate and unlatched it with a key he'd brought. The grate swung back, revealing darkness and the glint of moving water far below.

"That's the spring," he said. "It rises about fifty feet down, then flows west through the cave system until it joins the Grand Union Canal about a mile from here. Or at least, that's what the old maps suggest. No one's actually traced it."

Sarah knelt beside him, looking down into the hole. The water caught the torchlight and threw it back in patterns that seemed almost intentional, almost like writing. "Has anyone ever gone down there?"

"According to the records, three people tried," Catherine said. "In 1612, 1803, and 1951. None of them came back up."

"And you think there's something alive down there."

"I think," Daniel said slowly, "that there are things older than our categories. Older than alive or dead, natural or supernatural. The spring is a thing that persists, that wants things, that exchanges things. Whether it's alive in any sense we'd understand...
" He shrugged. "Does it matter?"

From the darkness below came a sound that wasn't water, wasn't stone settling, wasn't anything Sarah could name. It was a whisper and a scrape and a chord played on strings made of something other than gut or metal. Underneath it, Sarah detected strains of a calliope, wheezing and disjointed in the spaces between them.

It started in her skull, filling her sinuses with sweetness and agitation and longing, like a child walking into a fairground. It raised the hair on her arms and set her teeth on edge and made her heart soar the way it did in dreams when you realize you're flying.

Daniel's hand on her shoulder shocked her back into herself. Somehow she was almost at the edge of the hole.

"Jesus," she breathed.
"He has no power here," Catherine said quietly. "These are the old ways."

The sound came again, louder this time, and with it a smell that made Sarah gag - not decay exactly, but fullness, the smell of things that should never be brought forth, an intimate belch from deep within the earth's guts. It filled her with grief and longing and it took all her willpower to keep from crawling down towards that most beautiful entrance in the floor.
Catherine and Daniel exchanged a look. They climbed back up as the church bells began to toll eleven. Sarah emerged into the churchyard gasping, her lungs aching as if she'd been holding her breath the whole time. She rubbed her face, trying to shake the feeling of being ripped from a dream that she longed to return to.
The bells were wrong - not mechanically, but tonally. They rang in intervals that hurt to hear, that made her think of screaming and laughter and the sound a house makes when it's collapsing.

"That's the warning," Daniel said. "Every Embertide, the bells ring like that at eleven. The townsfolk know to stay home. It means the spring is stirring. It means we have until midnight to decide."

"Decide what?" Sarah demanded. "Whether to murder someone to appease a hole in the ground?"

"Whether to honour a contract," Catherine corrected. "Your family made a bargain centuries ago. The spring keeps Aylesbury safe, keeps the town prosperous, prevents floods and plagues and fires. In exchange, every seven years, we acknowledge that debt. We give what's required."

"A human life. A child."

"The lives of thousands," Daniel countered, "weighed against one. How is that different from any other calculation society makes?"

"We sacrifice young people to war. We sacrifice workers to dangerous jobs. We sacrifice the poor to poverty and the sick to inadequate healthcare. At least this sacrifice is chosen, deliberate. They're willing. It's better for them. At least it means something."

"They're children! This - this is monstrous."

"Yes," he agreed. "It is. But so is everything else, if you look at it closely enough."

Sarah backed away from them, toward the churchyard gate. "I won't do this. I won't choose someone to die."

"Then the spring will choose," Catherine said. Her voice was gentle, pitying, and somehow that was worse than if she'd been angry.
"You know that. And it won't be as gentle as we are."

Sarah ran.
She made it as far as Market Street before her legs gave out. She sat on a bench outside a closed Costa Coffee, her breath coming in ragged gasps, her heart hammering against her ribs.

Around her, the town was absolutely still. No wind, no traffic, no human sound. Just the wrongness of those bells, still ringing from St. Mary's, marking time toward midnight.

Her phone showed 11:17 PM. Forty-three minutes left.
She thought about getting in her car and driving. But where would she go? Back to London, to her empty flat and her dead mother? And what for, anyway? Her life there was over.

And would it even matter if she did run? Catherine said the spring followed bloodlines. Her great-aunt had documented the deaths of family members who'd fled - building collapses and car accidents and heart attacks that came too suddenly, too completely.

Her father had left Aylesbury before Sarah was born. He'd never spoken about his childhood, never brought her here. When she'd asked about her grandparents, he'd said they died when he was young and changed the subject.

He'd built his whole life elsewhere: London, started a career in accounting, a marriage, a daughter. Young, like he was racing against time. But he'd died at thirty-seven. Of a heart attack. It was a heart attack that his doctor said shouldn't have happened to someone so healthy.

Had that been the spring? Had it followed his blood for decades, taking payment for a debt that it owed? Catherine thought so, her Great Aunt Margery believed that she'd set this in motion.

And what about Great Aunt Margery's own death? No one had said how it had happened, but her dying so close to Embertide seemed connected - and it still hadn't been enough. What was it going to take to satisfy this thing if this was all real?

Sarah pulled out her phone and opened the map application. She zoomed in on the Old Town, looking at the street names: Market Street, Temple Street, Friar's Street, Kingsbury. Names that suggested commerce and religion and medieval power structures. And at the center, St. Mary's Church, built over a spring that was older than the concept of Christianity, older than England as a political entity.

She thought about the notebooks, about her great-aunt's careful documentation of seven-year cycles spanning decades. Her own discoveries of the awful consequences of noncompliance centuries ago. The pattern was there: provide the gift, maintain prosperity. Maintain the safety. Skip the gift, face consequences. Sooner or later, but inevitable. It was simple cause and effect, some cosmic level transaction and exchange, the brutal arithmetic of survival.

And at the heart of it was this terrible longing, this unquenchable need for a pure connection. She'd known this the second the sound had filled her ears, and known what it needed.

But it was also murder. Child killing.
There had to be another way.

Sarah stood up. 11:29 PM. Thirty-one minutes.
She walked back toward the Old Town, but not to St. Mary's. Instead, she turned down Friar's Street, following it to where it dead-ended at an ancient wall - part of the Norman defensive works, according to a heritage plaque. She'd seen something earlier, walking through the town, something she'd filed away as peculiar but not significant.

There: a modern door set into the old wall, painted blue and marked with the logo of Thames Water Authority. A maintenance entrance to the town's water system. And if

Aylesbury's water came from the underground springs, if the cave system connected, then perhaps -

She tried the door. Locked. The handle unexpected warm in her grasp. Jerking her hand away, she looked around for something to break the small window beside it, but before she could find anything, the door swung open on its own.

Sarah stood very still. The door hadn't been forced. The lock hadn't broken. It had simply opened, as if welcoming her in.

She stepped through.

From the streetlight she could make out stairs beyond that were metal and modern, descending into concrete-lined tunnels that smelled of damp and chlorine.

Sarah turned on her phone's torch and descended.

The stairs went deeper than she expected, switching back on themselves. After a couple of sharp turns, the steps became stone, the walls changing from modern concrete to old stone to raw limestone. Carved with those same spiral marks she'd seen in her cellar.

At the bottom, a metal walkway extended over a fast-flowing stream - not the spring itself, she thought, but one of the many channels that fed or drained it.

She followed the walkway, her footsteps clanging on the metal grating. The sound echoed strangely, multiplying and distorting until it sounded like many people walking, like a procession of the dead.

The tunnel branched and branched again. Sarah chose paths at random, guided only by the flow of water and a feeling she couldn't name - not exactly certainty, but something lodged in her reptile brain. A pull, like gravity but horizontal. Like something calling her home.

At 11:47 PM, she found it.

The chamber was natural limestone, cathedral-sized, its walls glittering with mineral deposits that caught her phone light and multiplied it into constellations. In the center, a pool of water so clear and still it looked solid, like black glass.

And in that pool, visible even from the edge of the chamber, something moved.

Not swimming. Not floating. Moving in a way that suggested intelligence and hunger and patience beyond human comprehension. It was too large to be single thing and too focused to be many. It was dark. Dense, but not black, solid but not tangible, with a presence as though somehow she was only seeing the part of it that intersected with normal space, with the reality she understood.

Sarah approached the edge of the pool. The water had no smell, no temperature, no reflection except the thing moving beneath its surface. Her phone's light penetrated the water but revealed nothing - no bottom, no walls, just endless depth and the thing that moved within it.

"Hello," she said. Her voice sounded small and strange in the vast chamber.

The thing didn't respond - not with words, not with movement. But the quality of the silence changed, became attentive. She felt it focusing on her the way you feel someone's gaze on the back of your neck.

"I'm Sarah Wickham. Margery's great-niece."

Still nothing, but the attention intensified. It was like being studied by something vast and alien, something that didn't quite understand what she was but was interested nonetheless.

"I understand what you want, what our families have promised you." She knelt at the pool's edge. The stone was wet and cold beneath her knees.

"But I can't give you what you're asking for. I can't choose someone to die. I can't be part of that."

The thing in the pool moved nearer to the surface. Sarah saw something that might have been an eye or a mouth or simply an opening, a place where the boundaries between substance and absence had worn thin. And looking at it, really looking at it, her mind began to fray a little at the seams to accommodate things that couldn't easily fit.

The thing in the pool wasn't a creature. It was something else. Something that existed in the spaces between categories, between alive and dead, between matter and thought. It was old in a way that made epochs seem like whimsy.

It had been here when the cave system was forming, when the water first found its way through the limestone, carving passages in the dark. It had been here so long that it had become part of the stone, part of the water, part of the deep earth itself.

And it was starving.

Not for food. Not blood. For acknowledgment. For energy. For connection to this, one of the worlds it inhabited, to envelop and consume and know that in this world the old ones still mattered, that they hadn't been forgotten in the darkness.

"But I can offer you something else," Sarah said. Her voice was steady, though her hands were shaking. "Myself. Not to die - I'm not a gift. But to stay. To be here with you, to maintain the connection. Isn't that what matters? That someone acknowledges you, remembers you, keeps the old agreements?"

The water rippled though there was no wind, no movement. From the pool came that sound she'd heard before, the not-music, the chord struck on inhuman strings. But this time it didn't hurt to hear. This time it sounded almost like a question.

"I don't know how long I'll live," Sarah continued. "Maybe thirty years, maybe fifty if I'm lucky. But for whatever time I have, I'll be your keeper. Yours. Willingly. No fighting. I'll maintain the house, tend your offerings. I'll sing you the old words. I'll let you drink from me. I'll be the connection between your world and ours."

The silence stretched. Sarah's phone showed 11:56 PM. Four minutes until midnight, until Embertide's culmination, until whatever the spring demanded came due.

"Please," she whispered. "Let me be enough."

The thing in the pool rose toward the surface, and Sarah saw it clearly for the first time.

It wasn't a creature. It was a thought given substance, a memory so old it had achieved physical form. It was hunger and inertia and the cold logic of deep places. It was every bargain ever made and every price ever paid. It was old beyond old, and it had been waiting not for sacrifice but for recognition. For someone to see it, speak to it, acknowledge its existence without trying to bargain or flee.

The water touched her fingertips where she'd braced her hands against the edge of the pool. It was cold enough to burn, and where it touched her, something changed. Not her flesh - her skin didn't freeze or dissolve. But something deeper shifted, some boundary in her she hadn't known existed.

She was still herself, still Sarah Wickham, thirty-six years old, divorced, motherless, kneeling in a cave beneath a town she'd never intended to live in.

But she was also connected now. Bound to this place, to this thing, to the deep water and the old agreements. She had been claimed and she belonged.

The church bells rang midnight, their tone pure and clear for the first time since sunset.

The thing in the pool sank back into darkness.

But it didn't release her. Sarah felt it there, beneath her skin, behind her eyes, in the spaces between her thoughts. Time passed, she lost track of how much, as she kneeled, suspended in the space between thoughts, aware of every sense, every shifting impulse.

She noticed faint crooning just at the threshold of sound, idly wondering how the creature produced it without a voice box until she realised that it was coming from her own. She eventually stood on legs that didn't feel entirely like her own and made her way back through the tunnels, following the water to the maintenance entrance.

She climbed the stairs and emerged into Friars Street just as the first light of dawn touched the rooftops. But the light looked different now. Thicker. As if she was seeing it through water.

The offerings were still on the doorsteps, but the painted symbols had faded to barely visible marks. The town was waking, ordinary sounds returning: a car starting, a door opening, someone calling to their cat.

Catherine Harrow was waiting outside Sarah's house, still wearing the clothes from the night before. When she saw Sarah, her face went pale. "What did you do?"

"I went to the spring," Sarah said. Her voice sounded distant to her own ears, as if she was speaking from underwater. "I spoke to it."

"And?"

"And I'm staying. I'm going to be the keeper, like Margery." Sarah pulled her keys from her pocket. They were cold and damp, though they'd been in her jacket the whole time. "But different. No more gifts. At least not for now. No more disappearances. Just acknowledgement. Company."

Catherine studied her face for a long moment. "It agreed to that?"

"I think it was what it wanted all along. We just didn't know how to ask."

"And if you're wrong? If in seven years it demands - "

"Then I'll deal with it in seven years." Sarah unlocked her door. The mechanism turned smoothly, but she felt it in her bones, felt the house recognizing her, welcoming her home. "For now, I need to sleep."

"Sarah - " Catherine reached out but didn't quite touch her. "Your eyes."

"What about them?"

"They're different. Darker. And something else. It's like there's water moving behind them."

Sarah went inside and locked the door without answering. She walked to the bathroom and looked in the mirror.

Catherine was right. Her eyes were darker. And when she looked closely, she could see something moving in them, something that caught the light and reflected it in patterns that looked almost like writing.

She went upstairs and slept for eighteen hours.

Part Five:

THE KEEPING

Sarah woke to darkness and the smell of limestone. For a moment she thought she was still in the cave, still kneeling at the edge of the pool. Then she realized she was in her great-aunt's bed, the heavy curtains drawn, the house silent around her.

She checked her phone: 11:34 PM. September 22nd. The second night of Embertide.

Her body ached in ways that had nothing to do with sleeping wrong. Her bones hurt. Her teeth hurt. When she ran her tongue over them, they felt too smooth, as if they'd been worn down by centuries of water.

She got up and went to the bathroom. In the mirror, her eyes were worse. The darkness had spread, the pupils dilating to swallow most of the iris. And the thing moving behind them was more obvious now, more active, pressing against the boundaries of her sight as if trying to see out.

Sarah touched the mirror and her reflection touched back, but half a second too late, as if the light had to travel through water to reach the glass.

She went downstairs. The house felt different - more present somehow, more aware. The shadows in the corners moved when she wasn't looking directly at them. The floorboards creaked in patterns that sounded almost like footsteps, almost like breathing.

In the kitchen, she found food she didn't remember buying: bread and cheese and apples, all fresh. On the table, a new notebook lay open to a blank page, a pen beside it.

Sarah sat down and began to write.

September 22nd 2022. The second day of Embertide. I went to the spring last night and made a bargain. Or perhaps the spring made me the bargain. It's hard to tell the difference anymore.

The connection is stronger than I expected. I can feel it beneath everything - this the house, spaces under the town, beneath this thin skin of civilization we've built over the old places. The spring is always there, cold and endlessly aware.

Great Aunt Margery was right about the keeping. It does require acknowledgment. But she was wrong about the form it needs. The spring doesn't want death. It wants life. It wants to be remembered, to be known. It's so lost. It wants to be connected.

I can give it that. I think I have to.

She wrote for hours, documenting everything she remembered from the cave, from the encounter with the thing in the pool. But the more she wrote, the less certain she became about what had actually happened. Had she spoken to it, or had it spoken through her? Had she made an offer, or had it made a demand? The memories shifted like water, never quite the same twice.

When she looked up, dawn was breaking. She'd spent the entire night writing. It was the third day.

She made tea and sat at the window, watching Bourbon Street wake up. People walked past - normal people, living normal lives, completely unaware of what lived beneath their feet. The woman with her stroller. A man walking his dog. Teenagers on their way to school.

They looked strange to her now. Too solid. Too bright. As if they were made of something more fragile than they realized, something that could dissolve in water if you left it too long.

Sarah went back to the cellar.

The jars on the shelves had changed. Or perhaps she was seeing them more clearly now. What she'd thought was a hand with too many joints was actually a hand with the right number of joints but arranged in a different configuration, optimized for swimming or grasping things in the dark. The honey-like substance wasn't moving on its own - it was responding to her presence, reaching toward her through the glass.

And the teeth. God, the teeth made sense now.

They were from people who'd gone into the spring over the centuries. People who'd been changed by the water, whose bodies had adapted to living in the dark and the cold and the pressure of deep places. The teeth had evolved to eat things that only existed down there, things that had no names in the language spoken above.

Sarah picked up one of the jars - the one containing what looked like preserved fruit but moved with obvious intelligence. She carried it upstairs and set it on the kitchen counter. Then she opened it.

The smell that came out was indescribable. Not rot, not decay, but intense ripeness. The smell of things becoming other things, of boundaries dissolving, of categories losing meaning.

The substance inside the jar flowed onto the counter, forming shapes - mouths, eyes, reaching tendrils. And Sarah understood that this was what her great-aunt had been doing down in the cellar all those years. Not preserving things, but tending to them. Maintaining the connection between the world above and the world below. Feeding the boundary, keeping it permeable.

She reached out and touched the substance.

It was cold and warm at the same time, viscous and mobile. It flowed up her arm, exploring her skin with hundreds of tiny mouths, each one tasting her, learning her, incorporating her into its understanding of what was possible.

And Sarah let it. Because she was a keeper now. And keeping meant being known and trusted by her charges. She was as much theirs as they were now hers.

Sarah spent the rest of the day in the cellar, cataloging the jars, reading the labels her great-aunt had written in that careful, precise hand. Each jar contained a piece of the spring, a sample of what lived down there. Some were recent - the dates on the labels went back only a decade or two. Others were ancient, the glass so old it had begun to flow, the contents preserved in ways that defied chemistry.

In the afternoon, on that third day of Embertide, Catherine came to the house.

Sarah opened the door to find her standing on the threshold, a basket in her hands. Catherine's face went pale when she saw Sarah, and she took an involuntary step backward.

"I brought bread," Catherine said quickly, brandishing her basket a little defensively. "And some things you'll need for the offering."

"Offering?"

"The one you're supposed to make tonight. At the spring. It's the third night - the night when the keepers traditionally renew the agreement."

Catherine looked past Sarah into the dark hallway, and Sarah saw her swallow hard, saw her hands tighten on the basket handle.

"Can I come in?"

Sarah stepped aside. The movement felt strange, her body responding to commands with a slight delay, as if the signals had to travel through water to reach her muscles. Catherine entered slowly, placing each foot carefully, as if testing the stability of the floor.

She set her basket on the kitchen table. Inside were loaves of bread that smelled of yeast and something else, something darker. Bunches of herbs Sarah didn't recognize - not rosemary or thyme or anything she'd seen in supermarkets, but plants with leaves that were too dark, too waxy, that seemed to absorb light rather than reflect it. And a small clay jar sealed with wax that had been stamped with a symbol Sarah recognized from the notebooks: a circle with three wavy lines, the sign for water.

"What's in the jar?" Sarah asked. Her voice sounded strange to her own ears - lower than it should be, with an echo underneath it, as if two voices were speaking slightly out of sync.

"Honey. But not from bees." Catherine set it down gently, as if it might break, or as if she was afraid to hold it too long. "Your great-aunt used to make it every seven years, during Embertide. She'd take it down to the spring and leave it there, and in the morning it would be gone. Consumed. Accepted."

She looked at Sarah's eyes and looked away quickly, her face going paler. "You need to do the same thing tonight. At midnight. It's part of the keeping."

"What happens if I don't?"

"I don't know. Margery never missed it." Catherine hesitated, still not meeting Sarah's gaze. "Sarah, are you - are you alright?"

"I'm adapting."

"To what?"

Sarah didn't answer immediately. How could she explain it in words that would make sense? She was adapting to the spring, to the thing that lived in it, to the connection that bound her to the deep water and the old stone. Every hour that passed, she felt less like herself and more like something else. Something older. Something that belonged to the darkness beneath Aylesbury.

Her skin had been changing. Not dramatically, not everywhere, but in patches - her hands, her feet, the skin over her sternum. It was paler than before, almost translucent, and when she held her hand up to the light, she could see through it to the bones beneath. The bones themselves were changing too. Growing denser in some places, more porous in others, adapting to pressure and cold and the demands of living in deep water.

And there were other changes. Her fingers were slightly webbed now, the skin between them extending further each hour. Her fingernails had thickened and darkened, and when she scratched at the kitchen counter absently, they left marks in the wood. Her teeth felt wrong in her mouth - too smooth, too sharp, arranged in her jaw at slightly different angles.

"Sarah," Catherine said again, and this time there was real fear in her voice. "Your eyes."
"What about them?"
"They're darker. Much darker than yesterday. And there's something moving in them. Behind them. Something that's watching me even when you're not looking at me."

She took another step back, toward the door. "This isn't right. This isn't what was supposed to happen. This has never happened to a keeper before. Not that I know of. You were supposed to be the keeper, not - not this."

"What's the difference?"

Catherine had no answer to that. She backed toward the door, her hand fumbling for the handle.

"Use the honey tonight. At midnight. And Sarah - " She paused, her face crumpling. "I'm sorry. We should have helped you. Should have warned you better. Should have - "

"Should have told me I'd dissolve into the spring?" Sarah smiled, and Catherine flinched at whatever she saw in that smile. "That eventually there'd be nothing left of me but a memory the water carries? That I'd spend whatever's left of my life becoming less human and more water, less Sarah and more spring?"

Catherine fled without answering.

That night, Sarah carried the jar of honey down to the cave. She knew the way without needing her phone's light, knew which passages to take, which turns would lead her to the chamber with the pool. The darkness didn't bother her anymore. She could see through it, or the thing moving behind her eyes could see through it, and it amounted to the same thing.

The spring was waiting, as she knew it would be.

Sarah knelt at the pool's edge and broke the seal on the jar. The substance inside wasn't honey - not really. It was thick and golden and moved with intention, but it smelled of deep earth and old bargains and things that had never been alive in any conventional sense.

She poured it into the water.

The spring accepted it immediately, the honey sinking without dispersing, forming shapes as it descended - mouths, eyes, hands reaching up toward the surface. And the thing in the pool rose to meet it, consuming it, incorporating it, using it to strengthen the connection between the world above and the world below.

Sarah felt that connection solidify in her own body. Felt it spreading through her blood, her bones, her nervous system. She was part of the spring now, part of the vast network of water and stone that ran beneath Aylesbury. She could feel the other springs, the other connections, spreading out like a web across the town and beyond.

And she could feel something else. Something her great-aunt had never written about in the notebooks, or had written about in code Sarah hadn't understood until now.

The spring was dying.

Not quickly. Not catastrophically. But slowly, over centuries, as the town above had grown and changed and covered the old places with concrete and steel. The connection between the world above and the world below was weakening, almost extinct. The agreements were mostly forgotten, the offerings neglected, the keepers dying without replacement.

Seven years ago, when Margery had refused to give the gift, it hadn't been the breaking of a chain. Not at first. It had waited, violence gathering momentum beneath, as the last desperate attempt of a dying system to survive, to demand the acknowledgment it needed to continue existing.

And Sarah had now given it that acknowledgment. But in doing so, she'd bound herself to something that was slowly fading, slowly dissolving back into the limestone and the dark water from which it had first emerged.

She could die with it. Not all at once, but gradually, as the spring faded. And when it finally died - in ten years, in fifty, in a hundred - she would die too, dissolved into the water, transformed into something that could survive in the deep places, adapted to living without light or warmth or the boundaries that made human life possible.

Sarah stood up. The water had left marks on her hands where she'd touched the jar - not burns, but changes. Her skin there was paler, smoother, almost translucent. She could see the veins beneath it, blue and dark and moving with something that wasn't entirely blood.

She went home. The fourth day of Embertide would begin at sunrise.

Part Six:

WHAT REMAINS

The fourth and final day of Embertide dawned cold and clear. Sarah woke to find her skin had changed overnight. Not dramatically, not everywhere, but in patches - her hands, her feet, the skin over her sternum. It was paler than before, almost translucent, and when she held her hand up to the light, she could see through it to the bones beneath.

The bones themselves were changing. Growing denser in some places, more porous in others, adapting to pressure and cold and the demands of living in deep water.

She wasn't afraid. Fear required a boundary between self and other, between what you were and what you might become. Sarah - who? - had lost that boundary. She was becoming something else, and fighting it seemed pointless. The spring had claimed her. She'd offered herself. This was simply what that meant.

Catherine came to the house at noon, bringing Daniel Becker with her. They stood on the threshold and stared at her.

"You need to see a doctor," Catherine said.
"What would I tell them?"
"That you're ill. That something's wrong."
"But nothing's wrong," Sarah said. "This is what I agreed to. This is what keeping means."

Daniel stepped forward, examining her hands without touching them. "How far has it progressed?"

"Far enough."
"Can you still - " He paused, choosing his words. "Can you still think? Still make decisions? Still be you?"

"I don't know," Sarah said. "Honestly, the line keeps moving. Sometimes I'm certain I'm still Sarah Wickham, still the person who drove here from London a week ago."

"Other times I'm not sure I was ever that person. I think I've always been this - the keeper, the thing that lives between the spring and the town, the boundary that has to be maintained."

Catherine's eyes filled with tears. "Margery wouldn't have wanted this for you. She wanted you to have a choice."

Sarah - Not Sarah - noticed an emotion flaring. Anger?

"Choice! To kill children. Or run, let things fall apart here, and die anyway?"

As quickly as it came, the feeling scudded away, a cloud in the wind. " I did have a choice. I made it."

"This isn't a choice. This is - " Catherine gestured helplessly at Sarah's translucent skin, her darkened eyes, the way she stood slightly wrong, as if gravity affected her differently now.

"This is possession. Corruption. This is the spring consuming you."

"Yes," Sarah agreed. "But it's better this way. Really, I understand now. Let it die? Let Aylesbury flood and crack and collapse? Let the thing in the deep water fade away after ten thousand years? No."

"Maybe that would be better."
"Better for whom?"

Catherine had no answer to that.

Daniel did. "Better for you. Better for your life, your future. Sarah – it's not too late. You don't have to do this"

Sarah. The name had started to feel like something she was wearing rather than something she was

She – or they? smiled at him "But this is my life. Remember, I couldn't walk away. The father tried. He died anyway."

Sarah looked at the hands, at the skin that was no longer entirely her skin. "At least this way, she is choosing. At least this way, we matter."
"You mattered before," Catherine said. "You matter now. You don't have to do this."

But Sarah was no longer listening. The spring was calling, exerting a pull toward the deep places. Embertide would end at midnight. Sarah needed to be there when it did, needed to seal the agreement, needed to complete the transformation.

Sarah - Who - Was closed the door on them and went to the cellar.

The jars had opened themselves. All of them. The contents had spilled out and flowed together, forming a pool on the dirt floor that looked exactly like the pool in the cave - dark and still and bottomless. Sarah knelt beside it and saw her reflection staring back at her.

Except it wasn't her reflection. It was her great-aunt.

Margery looked exactly as Sarah remembered her from the funeral - ancient, bent, her face carved into lines of sorrow and exhaustion. But her eyes were clear. And in them, Sarah could see the spring, could see the thing that lived in the deep water, could see the endless cycle of keeping and being kept that had sustained Aylesbury for centuries.

"I'm sorry," Margery's reflection said. "I should have warned you. Should have prepared you. But I was afraid you'd run, and we needed you too much."

"I know."

"It doesn't stop hurting. The transformation. Even after seventy years, even after you can't remember what it felt like to be entirely human, it doesn't stop hurting."

"I know."

"But you'll survive it. That's the terrible thing. You'll survive it and keep surviving it, year after year, until you can't remember why you thought any of it mattered. Until all that's left is the keeping."

Sarah reached out to touch the reflection, and her hand passed through the surface of the pool. The water was cold enough to burn. She felt it flowing up her arm, into her shoulder, into her chest. Felt it filling the spaces between her cells, replacing her blood with something older, something that had been flowing through limestone since before humans had a name for water.

"Will I forget who I was?" she asked, suddenly afraid.

"Eventually. But slowly. It's a mercy, in its way. By the time you're gone entirely, you won't remember there was ever anything to miss."

The reflection dissolved. Sarah pulled her arm out of the pool and watched as the translucent skin darkened, hardened, developed fine scales that caught the light like mother-of-pearl.

Six hours until midnight. Six hours until Embertide ended and the agreement was sealed.

She spent them reading her notebooks one last time, trying to memorize the words while she could still read them, while she could still understand the language of the world above.

Because she knew - the spring had shown her - that eventually she would forget. Eventually the words would stop making sense, would dissolve into the same incomprehensible patterns as the water moving in her eyes.

At eleven PM, she walked to St. Mary's for the last time as something recognizably human.

The church was empty. The town was silent. Even the cats had vanished. Sarah made her way to the back entrance, down the narrow steps, into the chamber with the grated opening.

But she didn't stop there. She continued down, following passages she'd never seen before but somehow knew, descending into the deep places where the limestone pressed close and the air tasted of minerals and time.
She reached the chamber with the pool at 11:57 PM.

The thing in the spring was waiting for her. It rose to the surface as she approached, like a lover awaiting their paramour, and Sarah saw it clearly for the first time - not the part of it that intersected with normal space, but all of it, the vast incomprehensible whole that extended into dimensions she didn't have names for.

It was beautiful. It was terrible. It was old beyond old and it was dying, had been dying for centuries, and her presence was the only thing keeping it alive.

Sarah knelt at the pool's edge as the church bells began to toll midnight.

She removed her shoes, her jacket, her clothes.

Stood naked at the edge of the water, her skin already more scales than flesh, her eyes dark and full of moving water, her bones dense and cold and ready for the pressure of deep places.

The bells rang twelve times. Embertide ended.

Sarah stepped into the pool.

The water embraced her. It was cold enough to stop a human heart, but Sarah's heart had already changed, had already adapted to function with less oxygen, with different chemistry, with the logic of things that lived in the dark.

She sank without struggling. Let the water fill her lungs, her throat, the spaces behind her eyes. Let it flow through her, around her, into her, until there was no difference between Sarah and the spring, between the keeper and the thing being kept.

She descended into darkness, into depths that had no bottom, into the vast network of caves and channels that ran beneath Aylesbury like veins, like thoughts, like the memory of water remembering what it meant to be alive.

And somewhere in that descent, somewhere in the cold and the dark and the pressure that should have crushed human bones, Sarah Wickham stopped being Sarah Wickham.

What remained was something older. Something that had waited ten thousand years to be remembered, to be acknowledged, to matter.

Something that would wait another ten thousand years if necessary, patient and cold and endlessly, endlessly hungry.

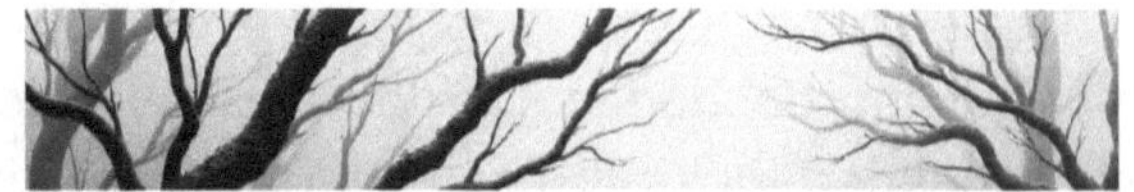

Epilogue:

Seven Years

September 25th, 2029.

Catherine Harrow stood outside 47 Bourbon Street, a basket in her hands. She'd been making this walk every three months for seven years, every equinox and solstice bringing bread and herbs and honey to the house that

Sarah had inherited, the house that had stood empty since the last night of Embertide in 2022.

Empty, but not abandoned. The door was always locked but never needed locking. The windows were always clean despite no one cleaning them. The garden grew wild but never overgrown, as if something was tending it in ways that didn't require human hands.

She knew without having to look, that every visit was observed by a hundred feline eyes, silent guardians and messengers watching from walls, undergrowth and parapets.

Catherine set the basket on the doorstep, beside the bowls that appeared there every Embertide - bowls filled with bread and salt and wine, offerings to something that no longer needed offerings but received them anyway, out of habit, out of memory, out of the endless cycle of keeping and being kept.

She turned to leave and stopped.

In the window - the one that looked out from what used to be the bedroom - stood a figure. Pale, translucent, neither entirely there nor entirely absent. It had Sarah's shape but not her substance. Its eyes were dark pools that reflected nothing, and in them Catherine imagined water moving, imagined the spring. Catherine stared at the thing that Sarah had become.

The figure raised one hand - webbed, scaled, beautiful in the way deep-sea creatures are beautiful - and placed it against the glass.

Catherine raised her own hand in response, though she couldn't bring herself to approach, couldn't make herself cross the threshold of what the house had become.

The figure watched her for a long moment. Then it turned and walked deeper into the house, into the darkness, descending toward the cellar where the pool waited, where the connection to the spring remained strong and cold and patient.

Catherine walked away. Behind her, Bourbon Street was silent except for the sound of running water - not from the pipes, not from the drains, but from somewhere deeper, somewhere beneath the town, where the spring flowed on and on and on, patient and cold and full of things that had once been human but weren't anymore.

Seven more years until the next Embertide. Seven more years until the debt came due again. Seven more years for the thing that had been Sarah to wait in the deep places, maintaining the connection, keeping the agreement, being the boundary and connection between the world above and the world below.

Catherine didn't look back. She couldn't.

But she felt it watching her all the way home - the spring, the thing in the spring, imagining the part of Sarah that remained conscious enough to remember what it meant to be kind, to be human, to stand in the sunlight and feel warmth on your skin.

That part was dying. Catherine knew, had seen it dying for seven years, watched it fade a little more each month, each visit, each offering placed on the doorstep of a house that was no longer a house but a threshold, a passage, a way down.

Soon there would be nothing left of Sarah at all. Just the keeper. Just the thing that lived between, that maintained the agreement, that fed the spring with its own gradual dissolution.

And after Sarah was gone entirely?

Catherine didn't know. Neither did Daniel, neither did anyone who remembered the old ways. The spring would need a new keeper eventually. Someone with the bloodline, someone with the gift, someone willing to descend into the dark and become something other than human.

Sarah had been the last Wickham. There was no one left. Only her and Daniel. And one day they would be gone and their lines with them.

Perhaps the spring would find another way. Perhaps it would adapt, evolve, continue in some new form. Or perhaps it would simply die, slowly, over centuries, taking Aylesbury with it - not in floods or fires but in gradual collapse, buildings sinking into sinkholes, people developing strange illnesses, children born with bones that weren't quite right, with eyes that reflected water, with fingers that were webbed and scaled and beautiful in ways that hurt to look at.

The thing in the deep water opened its mouth - or what had been a mouth, before it learned to breathe through its skin, before it learned to eat light and limestone and the slow dissolution of boundaries between self and other.
And it sang.

Not with a voice. Not with words.
But with the sound of water moving through stone, with the chord struck on strings made of dissolved bone and forgotten agreements, with the patient hunger of things that live in the dark and will outlive the light.

The song echoed up through the cellar, through the house, through the streets of the Old Town. And in every house, behind every twitching curtain, the families who remembered the old ways heard it and understood.

Catherine hurried home faster, locked her door and waited for morning.

TAMSIN PEAKE

FIN

About the Author

Tamsin Peake is a member of the **House of Sharky** collective, writing short horror, speculative fiction, and crime with a focus on the uncanny and the ethically uncomfortable.

Their work often explores how ordinary spaces become unstable, and how patterns of care, silence, and belief shape what people are willing to endure.

Tamsin's short fiction is set across the UK, with several stories rooted in Buckinghamshire. They publish new work regularly as part of an ongoing short horror series and works beyond.

Get alerted the moment our next book is
released:

More from the Short and Brutal Series

Tap Tap
The Allotment
Sing You To The Sea. (April 14th 2026)
The Tithing Ground (Title TBD)(Coming this May)
By The Throat (Coming this June)
The Work of Keeping (TBD)(Coming this July)
Sad Sack (Coming this August)
The Bearing of Witness (Coming this September)
The Keeper's Garden (Coming this October)
The Earth That Remembers (Coming this November)
Drowning Line (Coming this December)
The Counting (Title TBD. Coming early 2027)

www.houseofsharky.com